T

THE MYTH OF
THE TWIN

THE MYTH OF
THE TWIN

John Burnside

CAPE POETRY

First published 1994

1 3 5 7 9 10 8 6 4 2

Acknowledgements are due to the *Independent, Janus, New Writing* (Minerva),
*Pivot, PNR, Poetry Durham, Poetry Review, Stand, Sunday Times,
Times Literary Supplement* and *Verse*.

First published in the United Kingdom in 1994 by
Jonathan Cape
Random House, 20 Vauxhall Bridge Road, London SW1V 2SA

Random House Australia (Pty) Limited
20 Alfred Street, Milsons Point, Sydney,
New South Wales 2061, Australia

Random House New Zealand Limited
18 Poland Road, Glenfield,
Auckland 10, New Zealand

Random House South Africa (Pty) Limited
PO Box 337, Bergvlei, South Africa

Random House UK Limited Reg. No. 954009

A CIP catalogue record for this book
is available from the British Library

ISBN 0 224 03894 X

Typeset in Bembo by
SX Composing Ltd, Rayleigh, Essex
Printed and bound in Great Britain
by Mackays of Chatham PLC

CONTENTS

No estás, lo sé, fuera de mí, en el viento,
ni en el adiós, la tumba o la derrota,
ni en la nieve que suele prolongar
la sombra del olvido y el eco de jamás.

Canto a la soledad
Luis Cardoza y Aragón

HALLOWEEN

I have peeled the bark from the tree
to smell its ghost,
and walked the boundaries of ice and bone
where the parish returns to itself
in a flurry of snow;

I have learned to observe the winters:
the apples that fall for days
in abandoned yards,
the fernwork of ice and water
sealing me up with the dead
in misted rooms

as I come to define my place:
barn owls hunting in pairs along the hedge,
the smell of frost on the linen, the smell of leaves
and the whiteness that breeds in the flaked
leaf mould, like the first elusive threads
of unmade souls.

The village is over there, in a pool of bells,
and beyond that nothing,
or only the other versions of myself,
familiar and strange, and swaddled in their time
as I am, standing out beneath the moon
or stooping to a clutch of twigs and straw
to breathe a little life into the fire.

AVOIRDUPOIS

The weight of mercury and frost,
or the plover's weight of remorse
at the root of my tongue

when I stood in the polished hall
and my grandfather died by ounces
a door's-breadth away.

No one could measure his house:
the loads were too subtle, too fine:
the weight of hooks, the swish of gaberdine,

his ghosts come in to tea, still damp with rain,
stains in the books Aunt Eleanor had read
the year she died,

and where he lay, the weight of riverbeds:
the tide of shadows under Fulford burn
where fat trout swam like phantoms in the weeds

and where I saw him once, big and alive,
dabbling his hands in the water, as if he would lift
the fish of our dreams, the catch that would break
    the scales.

THE MYTH OF THE TWIN

Someone is still awake
in the night of my grandfather's house
with its curtains and potted palms
and its books full of beech leaves
pressed so the colours would stay,

and someone is having the dream
I had for weeks: out walking on the beach
I lifted a pebble and split it
open, like an apricot, to find
a live child hatched in the stone;

like radio, the whisper of the tide,
the feel of a pulse in the dark, when I stay up all night
and answers come, single and clear, like the calling of
    birds,
or the pull of the sea, when the moon sails high in the
    clouds
and I pick out the shapes on its surface: a handprint,
    an iris.

VARIATION ON A THEME OF WALLACE STEVENS

If I switched off the light
I would see him out in the yard,
tending a fire by the hedge,
raking the windfalls and leaves
from a different year,

a ghost in his smoke-coloured shirt
with his back to the house,
my double, from his looks: same age, same build,
the same clenched rage in his arms,
the same bright fear,

and I would be with him, looking at the dark,
but missing what he sees, or thinks he sees:
the sudden night, the blur of wind and rain,
the shadow in the woods that matches him
with nothing that is, and the nothing that is not there.

GRANDFATHER

Whenever he came to a place
he walked to its furthest edge
and found a borderland of wind and pines,

the field where gulls arrived
in winter, or the holy shade
of hellebore and fern.

Tracker of ditches; fence-minder, given to doubt
on clipped lawns and gravel drives
he wanted the light through the trees, the road to the
    coast,

roe-deer at evening, swimming in fields of wheat,
the half-imagined zenith where the kestrel
soars, in the once for all illuminate.

A PHOTOGRAPH OF MY
GRANDFATHER, c. 1961

There is something in his face
of death accepted:

a recognised form, like the shadow that comes to the door
and is only the cat,

the ghost of something
complex and remote.

Though now it is purely a journey he has to make
in a landscape he knows: the parklands and ripening fields

much deeper than they were, like painted glass,
and he knows what it is, to be travelling apart,

the sum of all the noons in empty rooms
and pauses in the rhythm of the crowd,

like being alone on a slow train that will not stop
till it reaches a coastline of sunlight and moving water.

MY GRANDPARENTS IN 1963

They had moved to the centre of things,
rounded and smooth, and closed upon themselves
like mushrooms,

or like the goblins in my books
they tended the fire in the hearth
and spoke in tongues.

A presence that had grown inside the house
they mingled, like moss and lichen, to suggest
the inextricable,

and sat together, bound in tea and starch,
unbending in the long accomplishment
of permanence, of choosing to be still.

THE DEAD

The life of another house
is what they seem,
the wind in a stranger's tree
at the end of the suburb,
a doorway filling with light
and the whisper of snow,

and I think they are still passing through:
weavers and children, and women with songs in their
      heads,
held on the air like an echo of bells or water;
I know who they are, condensed in the brick–dust and
      nettles,
I know how they lose their names
in the motionless earth

and how they return on these autumn
mornings, through the taste of smoke and loam,
a slow weight that shifts in my hands, a moment's
      warmth,
the glimmers of an afterlife deferred
for the promise that must be fulfilled
in the shaping of language.

LEARNING GAELIC

I have visions of anamnesis,
the handing down of an heirloom,
my mother's mother's language
matter-of-fact, and clear
as ice, or the cream of the well,

knowing the words I lack
have always existed:
a sound for the feel of a place,
for snowfalls that cover the roads
and little owls ascending through the trees,

a name for the gap between margins,
for siftings and scattered remains,
for rising at night, in the moments I share with the dead,
and making my place in their house, an echo, singing.

PISCES

She loved the wet whisper of silt
when tidewater seeped away
and the estuary rose to the town
through copper light,

a tender of glass and scales
and driftwood varnished with salt,
a circle she walked for miles
in search of shells,

picking starfish from a sheet
of silver tension, puzzled by the trails
of viscera, the threads of bloodless meat
and resurrected forms that had no names

but offered kinship, memory, regret,
a pulse between the water and her hand,
the feel of something old and buried deep,
heartbeat and vision quickening the sand.

NATURE TABLE

A litter of chestnuts and eggs;
a linnet's nest; a bread mould in a jar;
apples like magnets, wrapped in a film of rain.

I collected the windfalls and secrets,
beech-mast and old-man's-beard,
and scabs of stinkhorn in a handkerchief,

gathering myself in embryo
in what I took for nature, what I prized:
the badger's skull; the clutch of bristle-grass;

the tangle of cowhair and hoarfrost
picked from a fence; things shapeless or precise:
the slide of something waterish and quick

in leaf mould, or the mysteries I made
of home: its lacewing days; its nights of chrysalis.

NATURE POEM

The dark interior. But not the landscape
out beyond the fog

where others go,
and not the greenhouse with its dripping tap

and furred begonias,
but something that resembles both

and neither: a state of mind,
a sense of the mildew and fern

rankness in some corner of the soul
where wounds are healed,

a subtlety that lingers on the skin
through sleep or love, or when the hooded dead

reveal us all as shivers in the wind
gusted on woods and wheatfields after rain.

LOVE POEM

To think in the old language;
to waken at dawn
on the borders of dunlin and tern

with the same words, day after day,
remnants of healing and song
informing our house,

our only work, to keep in mind
the recipes and marginalia
of other times, the lore of clouds and tides,

or simply, when we come in from the dark,
to name things for the beauty of the sounds:
uisge; aran; oidhche; gealach; teine.

OCCASIONAL POEM

Charity Graepel, aged 2 months

Before the words for things
arrive in her mind,
there is only a sequence of echoes:
the wet eyes and rust-coloured hair,
the angle and pivot of bone
in the loose dark skin –

and she lives in a different state, where we
are fluid and indistinct,
figments of sound and nurture
flaring, then burning out,

and what she knows of dogs, or light,
or water, is a mystery to us,
who have them named and lost, a truth resolved
in the grammar that clothes and undermines our thought,
and shadows her wonder at this, the impossible world.

NAIAD

I never feared the leaf pools
deep in the woods,
black to the core of the earth
and veined with weed,

it was down at the village pond
where children drowned,
skating on waterish ice
then pulled into the cold

and swallowed. It took that much
to keep the houses still
around the green,
the playground abandoned for days,

and damp afternoons in school, where nothing said
could cancel out the shiver of desire,
a sudden girl with water in her hair
who stood up in the light and caught my eye.

NYMPH

Squinting out of the water,
the puddles that form in the yard
when it rains, or the colour of frogskin
that hangs on the afternoon air
along the canal,

this is the sister who died
when I rose to the light,
the vapour that dried on my skin, the film on my mind,
the anchor that drifted away
when they severed the cord.

I knew she was falling behind
in Latin and maths,
fading through months of chemistry and games
when I would have been down at the river
wading the ford,

the pull at my ankles like fingers, icy and quick
and strong enough to draw me
under, where my knowledge would become
a ripple, bleeding away
through gravel and weeds,

or the sudden, impersonal quiet
after a death,
the current slowed, the sense of giddiness,
the gap between one moment and the next
where nothing is that could have been a soul.

HYMN TO THE VIRGIN

When I stepped into the church on Lady Day,
the candles paled in the light
and she stood in a column of brightness,
anchored to the genus Lilium,

and somehow it always began:
the old sub-rational self
responding to a rhythm in the air
the way a swimmer merges with the sea.

Or later, after Assumption,
I walked home along the canal
shoulder-deep in sedge and meadowsweet,
and the space where I had left her was alive:
spawn-dark, silent, threaded with deceit,
cradled in a curvature of wings.

R . E .

Jesus remained for days
in the slow rain, under the trees
in Miss Allison's yard,

a fingerprint in the bricks
on the playground wall
was where he passed, a smudge of oil and blood
in the rust-coloured moss.

It was barely visible: you had to look
but everything showed him, even the crown of thorns
in a wood-pigeon's nest,

and the smell of a resurrection
arrived through the shirts
when the washing was left out all night
in the water and blackness.

CONVERSIONS

You remember the sand and rain
of church schools along the coast,
and children pinned to their books
by sudden doubt,

the numbers pointing away,
the whiteness of cosines and tangents
suggesting the colourless space behind a god,
a breeding void.

At dawn, when the nuns appeared
like magpies, they said the prayers
but everyone looked around
for the silent Christ,

and working the mission fields
they waited for storms to arrive,
lightning flashes, sheets of smoky rain,
the silence broken, mystery resumed.

FAITH

You would have unravelled a soul
from fishbones and lice,
from the brightness that seeps through the floor
when you walk in the dark,
and the birdless, indelible shadows
amongst the laburnum.

You would have imagined the physics
of limbo,
and paradise suburbs, where only the chosen exist,
the self made systematic: lawns and woods
and quiet houses
peopled with like minds.

In the morning you would have stood
alone, at the edge of the world
with your face to the light,
and God would become the camphor in a bush,
the whisper of something local and banal,
a personal event, which you would grasp,
inferred from the wind like a shiver of ash or pollen.

CURES

Our village has been spilled across the fields:
a litter of windows and porch-lights floating in snow,
and a darkness that seeps through the floors,
a current of cable and gas, of oakroot and bone,
and gravity, threading it all
with stillness and motion;

there are moments of random panic, out in the fields,
panic, and hooded joy at the weight of being;
there are old-fashioned cures on the flyleaf of every book
and people who scarcely know they are unwell
sit in their kitchens at midnight, watching the moon,
longing for tides and the secrets of mandragora.

STOCKHOLM SYNDROME

I

His choice is all or nothing:
cease to believe and the garden disappears,
elaeagnus fading into space,
nameless shrubs, unrealised nasturtiums.

But sometimes they let him
stand at the foot of the stairs
in the taste of smoke and the perfume of summer lawns,
and he knows there is something real

a step away: the sudden afternoon;
love letters written and posted all over town;
uniformed children, dizzy with the heat,
reading scriptures in a wooden room

and last year's household, foreign in the light,
its laundered curtains streaming in the breeze,
the windows darkened with the rounded shapes
of others: his successors; the deceived.

A theory of multiple drafts:
the self a charged miasma in the brain,
a web of messages, diminished now,

blank as the empty stockroom, where he lies
abandoned, with a table and a chair,
an empty glass, a single sheet of paper.

Passing the time, he learns the forms of rain,
gathers mists and drops to make a soul
from nothing, says the words

he learned in school: the litany of saints;
the three great mysteries;
the laws of motion. Later, they will come

with knives, or guns, masked with regret or tact:
not enemies, but strangers like himself,
as formless and informed behind the act.

THE HOUSE OF SOLITUDE

You have stepped inside for a moment,
leaving me quiet and strange
on this warm afternoon,
your footsteps chiming away
in the darkened hall,
moving towards that empty middle ground
where persons cease to exist, your words dissolved
in birdsong, your body erased,
and all of a sudden, I see why your bachelor's house
is peopled with mirrors,
I know how you find yourself melting, alone in the dark,
and how you are indisputable and sure
the moment you step from the shadows, clutching a book,
with something to show me: a riddle; a picture; a game.

DIALECT

There were different words for dust:
one for the powdered film
of shading on a closed room's
windowsills,

and one for the inch-thick
layer of talcum and fibre
under the bed,

but nothing to describe the vividness
of rain–dark fur and flesh that shaped and gloved
the body of a fox beside the road,

and nothing for the presence still to come,
when wind and sunlight fretted at the bone,
cutting towards the basics of the form:
the knitted spine, the hunter's steady grin.

THE NORTH

Mine is the other north:
villages waiting for gas by a restless sea,
the implications of a dying language,

the sense of a common usage to describe
a journey home, when others are at church,
the houses dark, the leafless apple trees,
a porch-light and the first wet flakes of snow,

or, further back, the point where night begins,
a thread of cold, a figment of the wind
that always finds an echo in my hands,

sidestreets where the dead are walking out
in twos and threes, sealed in a foreign tongue,
a grammar of old recipes and prayers
reserving names for things, when they are gone.

THE PIT TOWN IN WINTER

Everything would vanish in the snow,
fox bones and knuckles of coal
and dolls left out in the gardens,
red-mouthed and nude.

We shovelled and swept the paths,
but they melted away in the night
and the cars stood buried and dumb
on Fulford Road.

We might as well be lost, she said;
but I felt the neighbours dreaming in the dark,
and saw them wrapped in overcoats and scarves
on Sundays: careful, narrow-footed souls,
become the creatures of a sudden light,
amazed at how mysterious they were.

RUNNING AWAY

I wanted to travel eastwards,
braving the radio blizzards
of Stockholm and Oslo,
finding, at last, the lime-flavoured gap
of Vienna.

That was September: a blue wind turning the leaves
and the streetlamps crimson and gold
on Victoria Road;
I hunkered down under a lilac
and waited for day

but they found me at two in the morning, cold to the
    bone,
and the distance grew empty and strange, like the churches
    on maps,
the glitter of something else I would never find,
like the perfume of home,
or the still pools of love and possession.

LAMPLIGHTER

I honour and hide this blood:
the flavour of coal on my skin,
and the gap in the stone
like a small resurrection of frogs.

My grandfather stands in the hall
with his lantern and gloves,
still dusted with the blue of afternoon
he has wandered the length of the town
like a man in a trance.

He is looking for something he lost
in a clouded shaft,
the stranger he carried for hours, then left behind,
the dead weight that renders him whole.

Sometimes he digs so deeply in the vein
that ghosts appear, small curls of shell and fern;
sometimes he breathes the carbon of a time
before us all; and once, when he was given up for lost,
he drew a film of sulphur from the wall
as absolute and ageless as the stars
that pale when he goes out to light the lamps.

OWLPEN

The Arts and Crafts mosaic
has crumbled from the wall
in small bright sherds,

water and ivy
seep through the broken panes
in the painted glass,

but this is my only parish,
a space without chairs or bells
and an altar that smells of mice
in the wet-weather dark,

my only church this half an hour
of shelter in a sudden fall of rain,
this moment, with the presence at my back,
of knowing when I turn there will be nothing.

HOME FARM

I am thinking of hedges and orchards,
the paths I could walk in the dark
from field to field

and a silence about the house
like a wider self,
a lifelong, unlaboured attunement,

rehearsing the names of crossroads,
breeds of sheep, varieties of pear,
words to exchange with a neighbour for no good cause

but the making and sharing of sounds,
the subtle replacement of meaning
with pauses and gestures,

a form of courtesy, the marking out of bounds
we do not choose, and take so long to measure.

IN LANCASHIRE

They have left the porch lights burning
in Kirkham and Fleetwood,
and people are still driving home
to their gardens of dew,
to gaps in the stairwell
where something has just disappeared,

the way they once believed
the angel was a presence in the room
that bled away the moment you came in,
they think it harbours something of themselves
that might be lost
or not quite understood,

and they look to the blur of the mirror
for something more,
a fraction of the dark that echoes back
the people from a textbook, who exist
when all their dreams are parsed and set aside:
completed selves, like people from a game,

lifting their heads from the problem they wanted to solve
and suddenly becoming what they are:
possessed of being, absent by design,
tuned to the pitch of navelwort and kelp,
to the candle-stub melting in ice
and the uses of madder.

AN OPERATING SYSTEM

Like a room you discover by chance
– one of those rooms in the basement
where nobody goes,

the closed air softly magnetic
and off-sweet, like a summer of mint and privet,
the locked machine singing away,

maintaining the fabric, the life's work of apples and bees,
absorbing the weight of the bonfires you find at dawn,
the last charred pages of letters and magazines,
the fall of leaves, the clutch of rabbit bones –

there is another fastness in the mind
wide as a room, but tiny, and self-contained,
like the wren's egg you find in a smokebush, surprising
    and warm,
a thread of the fabric, and almost your only clue.

A MERCHANT'S HOUSE,
WEST FRIESLAND

It must be renewed each day, this wealth
of perfume and appraisal,
sacks of bark and seed, nutmegs and cloves,
not mere commodities, but goods, rich as the songs
that rise through warmth and sleep.
Beyond the glass, infinity's
a commonplace: the broad grey lines
of iced canals and skaters
meeting in the distance that appears
on antique maps. The pure formalities
of loss and gain
become redundant in a moment's lived
detachment, in the whisper of the wind
on frosted glass, the spice of transience.

ULEY, GLOS

The moonlight is suddenly large:
a brightness on the fields that only shows
when this house dims

and something clearer rises
through the parish I know by heart,
bricks and glass, the dead immersed in stone,
subtle erasures, siftings of blood and bone,

as if this was the story of a place
that I could tell without impediment:
first thought, then form, a drift of native souls
scattered across the land like seed or snow,

ordered and lost; a sieve of consciousness
the making of this commonplace domain:
respected borders, marriages and births,
the giving up and taking on of names.

DUNDEE

The streets are waiting for a snow
that never falls:
too close to the water,
too muffled in the afterwarmth of jute,
the houses on Roseangle
opt for miraculous frosts
and the feeling of space that comes
in the gleam of day
when you step outside for the milk
or the morning post
and it seems as if a closeness in the mind
had opened and flowered:
the corners sudden and tender, the light immense,
the one who stands here proven after all.

DARK GREEN

There is always a place on the way
where the path curls into the dark,

into the smell of dust
and the stillness of nettles.

There is always a litter of stones
or a broken roof

a few steps into the shade;
an empty skull, a ribcage stitched with grass,

barely a trace of the vapour that had lived
before you came:

a remnant of mucus and water, hatched on a bone,
like the silver-and-eggshell perfume after a birth,

or the whisper that swells and recedes in the quick of your
    mind
when you wake in the day, and the bright dream runs on
    without you.

SEPTEMBER EVENING;
DEER AT BIG BASIN

When they talk about angels in books
I think what they mean is this sudden
arrival: this gift of an alien country
we guessed all along,

and how these deer are moving in the dark,
bound to the silence, finding our scent in their way
and making us strange, making us all that we are
in the fall of the light,

as if we had entered the myth
of one who is risen, and one who is left behind
in the gap that remains,

a story that gives us the questions we wanted to ask,
and a sense of our presence as creatures,
about to be touched.

CREDO

I almost believe the meadows will return,
glistening under the moon, caressed by owls,
charted for years by foxes and their young;

I half-expect a silence I could touch
to form at nightfall over love and prayers
when each soft household folds into the dark;

I think of sandstone walls outside the town:
those slow chromatographs of frost and moss
where I studied the motion of light
and the colours of water;

but more than anything, I know the dead
will gather to our fires at Halloween,
and we will meet them, tongue-tied and beguiled,
lighting up these parishes for miles.

FORM

A new moon recovers the hare
from its absence in grass and water.

They have built me a fire in the yard,
a childhood laid in seams
of ash and fur,
and I sit at the window, sick
with measles: the window ajar,
the wet light fledging the glass
and a ribbon of wind through the darkness
touching my hands.
I have something to remember and erase,
the quick of something colourless and pure,
and empty as the centre of the flame
before it falters, pulled into the web
of hessian and broken apple boughs,
and slow weights dropping through, like nails or coins.

PUBERTY

The water that left my hands
immaculate; the stolen jay's-egg
crushed against my tongue

and dead men's fingers
clutching through the leaves;

or the winter I woke alone
and naked, night after night,
in a house of owls:

the round, maternal faces
sweeping through a cloud of mint and starch

a moment before I woke, then all day long
in the whisper of silk when Miss Cameron bent to my
    desk
and I tasted the almost-contact of her hair
rich with the mingled flavours of milk and frost.

EPISTEMOLOGY

I begin to suspect there are creatures
to match us, under the earth:

fish in the dew-ponds
dreaming us alive,

moles in a velvet landscape of thuds and sighs
decoding a muffled existence they would guess

was music, or a story being told
in cipher.
             We are discontinuous

but knowable, after a fashion,
in such a world:

a shiver of noise at the spine, a fragment of scent,
a middle-ground of faith and hesitance,

touched by the same rain,
clenched in the same bright frost.

A PEN FRIEND

A child's imagining,
that someone could be twinned
across those miles,
tuned to the same dark channel
of guesswork and song,

a real-time instance of myself
achieved elsewhere,
a boy in a fishmonger's stripes
with milt on his fingers
or caked blood under his nails,

a mutuality
of love and fear,
similar patience, identical maps and toys,
the horse in each attic
awake in the motherless dark.

THE SOUL FRIEND

This is the fish-coloured bible,
buried in the garden, under webs
of bone and rain,

the love letter scratched on a desk,
then smoothed away
in waves of sweat and grain,

the taste of hallelujah in the dark
when the prayer for the dead is begun
and the candles burn out on the altar
like daffodils melting,

and this is the form you describe
as witness, like the child you used to be,
standing all day in the playground, measuring frost,
inventing a father from hearsay and fragments of Latin.

A LO MEJOR, SOY OTRO

I am standing behind the door
at the foot of the stairs
on the first day of term.

I am ready for school
in my raincoat
and navy-blue gloves,

forgetting the dream
where I wake in a fall of snow
and go with the others,

forgetting the smoke and the linen,
the footpath of ashes and hair,
the caskets of lice,

and forgetting the measureless need
to be myself,
to be myself alone, not someone else,

and never the boy
with the number stamped on his arm,
the one in the film
with my face, in my raincoat and gloves.

LAPSED

I know how difficult I am
coming from the garden and the rain
with the warmth in my fingers
of something I cannot describe.

A child, I had visions of Christ
in the afternoon sun,
a risen body standing in the heat
like the Jesus who would not be touched

and resembled a gardener. That presence dissolved,
I cling to the relics I find
in water and loam,

the rusted nails and sherds of *sang de boeuf*,
and rags of linen where my face appears,
indelible, in scabs of blood and matter.

THE RESURRECTION

Something is green in the house
of a sudden:
all morning I finger the windows,
revealing the moisture, the heartbeat that rises through
    stone,

and later, in the stillness after Mass,
I guess what it might have been
to discover the tomb:
the empty linen printed with a stain

of presence, like a broken chrysalid,
where something has struggled loose, through
    remembrance and pain,
and the angel, a handsbreadth away,
in the blood-scented shade,
a breathless, impossible being, diverting my gaze
from that which is risen, the living, unnameable God.

ANGELS EYES

Under the curve of the sickle
a region of speedwell and lime
where birds disappear,

and rainwater sipped from the grass
becoming the song in your mouth
of summers and endings,

where angels arrive through the hedge,
and the dead from your schooldays
are waking through nettles and elms,

or walking away in the corn, and leaving no trace
save the grey of a bruise on your wrist
and the blur in your eyes

where someone reached out from a drowning, a lifetime
    ago,
and held you for minutes, before you could shake yourself
    free.

PRE-BOTANICAL

The churchyards are secret cures:
milk-coloured seeds to unravel eczema and blindness,
sudden petals, veined with blood and rain.

And surely the dead are pagan,
huddled in stone, or waiting their turn in the light,
surely their names and faces have dissolved
in something pure: an element, a source,

the tales they would tell, if they could,
of absence or loss,
the bathed flesh buried in moss, and the frost of
    unknowing.

THE ASTRONOMERS' DISTRICT

Autumn arrived in the night:
a slow wind changing the park
from silver to blue,

then weeks of falling leaves and frosted lawns,
the city quiet and old with blackbirds and medlars:
a world you could name in Latin.

When snow came, I watched the children
walking to school,
their pockets full of compasses and pins
and clutches of moss, to be named and discarded later,

the fragments of a life that would be proved
by midnight, when the telescope was clear
and the cool stars flowed into place
through an infinite blackness.

PASSION

You are measuring something cold
in the still of the yard

this weekday afternoon, when the trees
are small and abandoned;

a faint world written in smoke
hangs at your back like the point in a dream

you forget, and the distance begins
as if it were something resumed, like a game or a song,

or the story you tell for no reason, that no one will hear:
a riddle, a myth,

the passion you think you have feigned
for years, and those fragments of prayer

that bleed through your thoughts in the gold of the
    afternoon,
when you guess what it was that was difficult all along.

THE MYTH OF THE TWIN

Say it moved when you moved:
a softness that rose in the ground
when you walked, or a give in your step,
the substance that Virgil saw
in the shadows under our feet;

and say it was out there, out in the snow,
meshed with the birdsong and light
the way things are real: a blackbird, a scribble of thorns,
a quickening into the moment, the present tense,

and the way that a stumbling or sudden
rooting in authenticity is not
the revelation of a foreign place,
but emptiness, a stillness in the frost,
the silence that stands in the birchwoods, the common
    soul.

IN AVON

In Spring we can taste the river
as far as our bed.
We dream of frogs and silt
in the brackish dark,
then wake in the daylight
prepared for a transformation.

*

Or we sit in the loam-flavoured shadows
under the trees
and watch for hours, for what the river brings:
the flat eyes and glimpses of bronze
in the bottleglass weeds,
the rumours of ourselves that come in waves,
the spun lights and splinters of naming.

*

The river is a life we do not use:
the dreams we half-remember, then forget,
a shimmer of sequins and tinsel
dissolving, like the vein of starch and yeast
we take for love.

*

Away from the bank, we sit in the standstill of home,
with nothing to wait for, and nothing to understand;
the river is flowing away and remaining in place,
sifted by summer, darkened by foxes and owls;
in autumn the leaves bleed out through a wavering skin,
seed finds its level, fishbones and fleece decay.

*

All winter it changes. We find it again and again.

THE SOLITARY IN AUTUMN

I am standing out in the yard
at the end of October,
building a fire of drifted leaves and twigs,
letters for kindling, apples amongst the flames,
the last of summer, dropping through the embers.

There is that perfume in the shade
that is almost viburnum,
traces of snow and water in the light,
a blankness along the canal
that waits to be filled

and, given the silence, given the promise of frost,
I might have welcomed this as something else:
the taste of windfalls moving on the stream
a faint god's partial emergence
through willow and alder.

The riverbank darkens and fades.
The garden recovers its creatures: slow worms and frogs
and blackbirds sifting the dead
in the still of the damsons.
Across the river, evening bleeds the trees,

my neighbour's garden blurs to smoke and rain;
sometimes I think that someone else is there,
standing in his own yard, raking leaves,
or bending to a clutch of twigs and straw
to breathe a little life into the fire.